My Classic Stories

Goldilocks and the Three Bears

This book belongs to

Age -----------

Enjoy this book,
love from

Goldilocks and the Three Bears

This edition first published in 2013 by Ginger Fox Ltd
Copyright © 2013 Ginger Fox Ltd

Published in the UK by:
Ginger Fox Ltd
Stirling House, College Road
Cheltenham GL53 7HY
United Kingdom

www.gingerfox.co.uk

Retold by Nina Filipek
Illustrated by Jacqueline East

ISBN: 978-1-909290-05-1

10 9 8 7 6 5 4 3 2 1

Printed and bound in China.

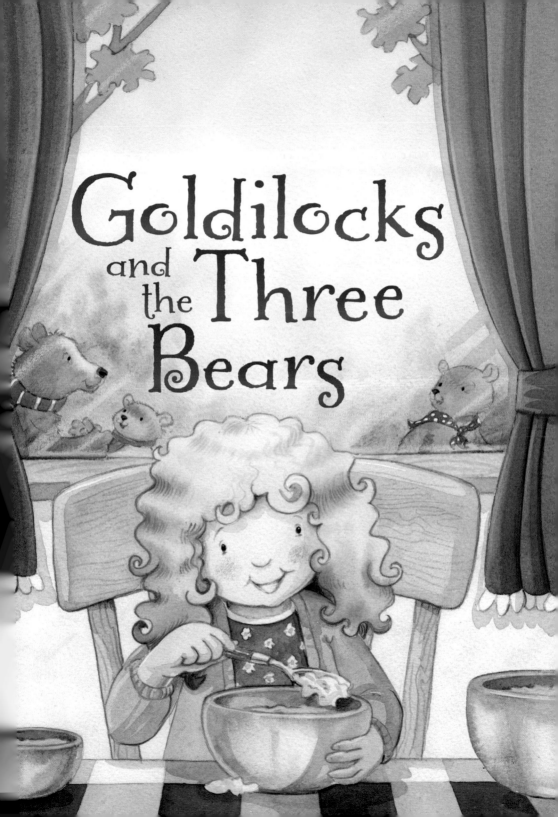

Goldilocks and the Three Bears

Once upon a time there were three bears –
daddy bear, mummy bear and baby bear.

One morning, mummy bear made some
porridge for breakfast.

She poured it into three bowls – a big bowl, a middle-sized bowl and a little bowl.

The porridge was too hot to eat, so the three bears decided to go for a walk while it cooled down.

Goldilocks was
also out walking
in the forest that
same morning. She
spotted the three
bears' cottage.

She knocked on the door, but no one replied.

She looked through the window. She could see
that no one was at home so she went inside.

Goldilocks was a very nosy little girl!

When Goldilocks saw the porridge on the table she felt hungry.

She tasted the porridge in the biggest bowl – but it was too hot.

Next, she tasted the porridge in the middle-sized bowl – but it was too cold.

Then she tasted the porridge in the little bowl. It was just right – so she ate it all up!

When she had finished the porridge, Goldilocks saw three chairs in front of the fireplace.

She sat in the biggest chair – but it was too high.

Next, she sat in the middle-sized chair – but it was too low.

Then she sat in the little chair – and it was just right.

But Goldilocks was too heavy, and the little chair broke!

13

Now Goldilocks was feeling tired, so she climbed the stairs up to the bedroom.

She lay down on the
biggest bed –
but it was too hard.

Next, she tried the **middle**-sized bed – but it was too soft.

Then she tried the littlest bed – and it was just right. Goldilocks snuggled under the covers and was soon fast asleep!

Downstairs, the three
bears had returned home.
They knew immediately that
someone had been in their cottage.

"I'm sure I closed the door!"

said daddy bear.

The three bears saw the porridge
bowls on the table.

"Someone's been eating
my porridge!" said daddy bear in
a big booming
voice.

"Someone's been eating
my porridge!" said mummy bear in
a middle-sized voice.

"Someone's been eating my porridge!"

cried baby bear in a
squeaky little voice,

"and they've eaten it all up!"

Then the three bears saw the chairs
by the fireplace.

"Someone's been sitting
in my chair!"

said daddy bear in a
big booming voice.

"Someone's been sitting in my chair!"

said mummy bear in a **middle**-sized voice.

"Someone's been sitting in my chair!"

cried baby bear in a squeaky little voice,

"and they've broken it!"

Next, the bears climbed the stairs up to their bedroom.

"Someone's been sleeping in my bed!" said daddy bear in a **big** booming voice.

"Someone's been sleeping in my bed!" said mummy bear in a **middle**-sized voice.

"Someone's been sleeping in my bed!" cried baby bear in a squeaky little **voice**,

"and she's still there!"

At that very moment, Goldilocks woke
up and saw the three bears staring at her.

She had never been so frightened!

She leapt out of bed and
ran as fast as her legs could
carry her, out of the door,
through the forest, and far, far
away from the three bears' cottage.

Goldilocks never went there
again and everyone lived
happily ever after.

Can you remember?

Now that you have read the story, try
to answer these questions about it.

1. What did mummy bear
make for breakfast?

2. Why did the three bears
go for a walk?

3. Why didn't Goldilocks like daddy bear's bed?

4. Whose chair did
Goldilocks break?

5. "What did I
say when I saw
my porridge had
been eaten?"

6. Why do you think
Goldilocks never visited the
bears' cottage again?

Did you spot?

Goldilocks had a good look in and around the three bears' cottage, but how well did you look? See if you can find all these things in the story.

1. Two butterflies fluttering by a tree?

2. A sleepy owl?

3. Two bookends shaped like animals?

4. There is a bee on baby bear's bib, but how many other bees can you spot in the story?

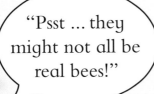

"Psst ... they might not all be real bees!"

5. Which of baby bear's toys was by his bed?

6. What time is it on the clock in the living room?

True or false?

Can you answer these true or false questions correctly?

1. The bears liked porridge.

True or false?

2. Goldilocks was a nosy girl. **True or false?**

3. Daddy bear had
   a squeaky little voice. **True or false?**

4. Baby bear kept a football under his bed.

True or false?

5. The bears scared Goldilocks.

True or false?

Such a puzzle ...

Look carefully at the pictures below
and then try to answer the questions.

1. Whose chair was this?

2. Whose slippers were these?

3. What was happening in this part of the story?

4. What is different about daddy bear in this picture?

My Classic Stories

Complete your collection ...

The Ugly Duckling

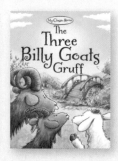

The Three Billy Goats Gruff

Hansel and Gretel

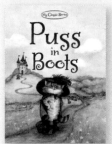

Puss in Boots

Little Red Riding Hood

Jack and the Beanstalk

Cinderella

The Gingerbread Man

The Emperor's New Clothes

Goldilocks and the Three Bears

Rapunzel

The Three Little Pigs

"Which one will you read next?"